TRAPPED IN MOONSHINE MINE

TRAPPED IN MOONSHINE MINE

STORIES FROM THE MOUNTAINS OF THE LAKE DISTRICT

CHRIS RODGERS

CRESCENT HOUSE

CHRIS RODGERS

First published in 2017 by **Crescent House**, an imprint of Vertebrate Publishing.

Crescent House
Crescent House, 228 Psalter Lane, Sheffield S11 8UT UK.

A CIP record for this book is available from the British Library.

ISBN 9781909461529

10 9 8 7 6 5 4 3 2 1

Chapter page and cover illustrations by Simon Norris.

Designed and set in Baskerville MT, Komika Text Tight and SF Slapstick Comic
by Nathan Ryder – Vertebrate Publishing.

Crescent House is committed to printing on paper from sustainable sources.

Printed and bound in Poland.

CONTENTS

Chris Rodgers was born in Preston in 1950, and spent most of his working life in local government.

Chris's writing is inspired by his love of walking on the fells of the Lake District and also farther afield in Wales and Scotland. His storytelling follows a long tradition of picking up on historical themes and ancient places in the Lake District, and he has written numerous articles including a feature on climbing Scafell via Lord's Rake, for *Trail* magazine.

Chris is married to Liz and they have two grown-up children. He has told many of his real-life adventures to his grandchildren, who always ask if they are really true stories.

FOR HARRY AND THOMAS WHO HEARD
THESE STORIES FIRST.

FOR JESSICA AND CALEB WHO
ENJOYED THEM TOO.

THE WILD BOAR OF TRUSMADOOR

Chapter One

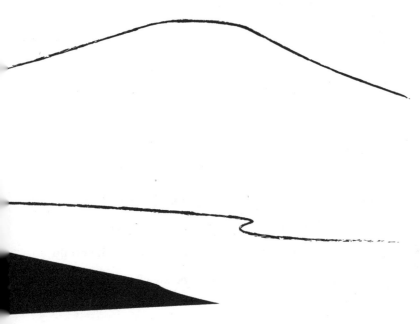

Many, many years ago The Wild Boar of Trusmadoor made its home in the faraway lands of the northern Lake District known as 'Back o' Skiddaw'. Also roaming these lands was a rugged old packhorse woman known only as 'Packwoman'. She used to travel with her pony through the hills from the small market town of Keswick to distant farms in Longlands and Fellside, selling her goods. She knew the area well, often making her way through the valleys of Burntod Gill and Trusmadoor to shorten her journey.

In those days, a journey to town would be a very rare occasion and a visit from Packwoman to their lonely homes was welcome. Selling her goods brought her very little money; she usually exchanged them for food from the farms. She would trade rope, leather goods, buckets, mops, rakes and spade heads, and even toys for the children. Although she left the farms with very little money she was happy enough with the butter, eggs, bacon and other farm produce she could easily sell at the marketplace in Keswick.

It was always the journey back to Keswick that was the most hazardous. The foxes, wolves and wild boar could smell the food that her pony carried. Sometimes she would take a higher route over the hilltops of Longlands and Knott to avoid the worst of the scavenging animals. On fine, moonlit nights this was no trouble, but one particular evening, after a long hot day, a storm was starting to brew up. Packwoman knew it would be foolish to risk travelling over the hilltops. She would have to take the lower route through the valleys of Trusmadoor and by Burntod Gill.

As she made her way through the gloom, she could hear screeches and howls from the wild animals and birds that hunted there. To add to her distress, the rumbles of thunder were getting nearer. She knew the shiver of the pony was not because of the chill of the night. It was too warm and muggy. Even though she had not heard the terrifying high-pitched grunt, Packwoman knew the pony had sensed the closeness of the dreaded wild boar. She was aware the animal was playing a clever game; he would be silent until close enough to pounce on them.

Suddenly the wild boar let out the most tremendous, deafening cry: 'ROOAAARRRR!' At the same time the night sky was lit up by a magnificent flash of lightning as she saw him rise up on his hind legs, his enormous white tusks gleaming. Then all was dark and quiet. She waited for another roar from the wild boar but there was none. In the next flash of lightning she saw him, lying motionless on the ground, as still as a stone, his huge mouth hanging open. Grabbing the pony's bridle, her heart pounding, she ran as swiftly as she could, tripping and stumbling, down the rocky path. And still there was not a murmur or movement from the wild boar. To her surprise and relief, he had not followed.

Chapter Two

After that night she didn't want to visit the Back o' Skiddaw ever again. It was only after a chance meeting at the market in Keswick, with one of the shepherds from the hills, that she became brave enough to venture there once more. He had told her that no one had seen or heard the wild boar since that stormy night.

For her next visit, she waited until the weather forecast was good and planned to return in daylight hours.

When she arrived on the hilltops she could not resist a look down into the valley of Trusmadoor. She could only vaguely remember the spot where she had seen the wild boar. It was a bright, sunny day and out of curiosity she ventured down the hillside. Arriving at the foot of the gully, she thought she could see the shape of a wild boar in the distance. After a brief pause, and with the pony trying to pull in the opposite direction, she edged slowly forwards. She was very close and still the creature did not move or turn towards her. She saw that the great wild boar had been turned to stone. It was then that she remembered the legendary tale, told to her by an old shepherd of the Uldale Fells, when she was a child. According to this tale, the last wild boar in England would be turned to stone by a bolt of lightning. And that night, the night of the storm, Packwoman had witnessed in Trusmadoor just what the tale had foretold.

To this day if you happen to pass through that remote valley, fear not! It is not a grisly wild animal you see crouching there, but the fossilised stone mass of the great wild boar, who met his fateful end in Trusmadoor.

A GHOSTLY FERRY TALE

Chapter One

'Let's light the campfire!' said Tom. 'Then we can have some soup with the sandwiches.' Harry had never known Tom bother about soup before.

'If we light a fire we can't leave camp until it's put out,' he said. 'Do you want to go out in the boat today or not?'

'Course I do!' yelled Tom.

'Good, then we can light a fire when we get back.'

This was the moment Harry and Tom had been dreaming about ever since they had planned the camping trip. This year they were on a campsite in the Lake District. Their parents were staying on a caravan site nearby. The boys had been practising camping in their garden and now it was for real. Harry was fourteen and, now that Tom was twelve, their parents were happy for them to camp on their own for the very first time.

Careful preparations had been made all spring for this trip. The *Curlew*, their rowing boat, was thoroughly cleaned and polished and was now spotless. As the long-awaited day finally came, Harry's detailed list was checked and double-checked and, with the car packed full to the brim, at long last they were off.

A few hours later they arrived at the campsite on the west shore of Lake Windermere close to a place called Claife Heights. The *Curlew* was tied to a tree by the shore of the lake, and the camp was set up. The boys waved their parents off knowing they were staying close by and were only a phone call away. They were finally camping all by themselves in the wild.

Now they were alone, their adventure was to begin. Although they could not wait to get the boat launched, Harry was determined to keep some form of order. It was already past their normal lunchtime and with their little squabble over, the first camp meal was eaten without the need of a campfire. All was left tidy; they even washed the tumblers in the nearby stream.

Taking some of Grandma's home-made flapjacks and drinks, they put on their life jackets and untied the *Curlew*, and carefully launched the boat over the stony bottom of the lake. Harry used one of the oars as a punt to get started, and they were afloat at last, rowing on Windermere, the largest natural lake in England.

Lake Windermere was so big that it had lots of little islands scattered about among it. Tom and Harry were heading towards Belle Isle, the largest of the lake's eighteen islands. It appeared so huge that it seemed to blend in with the hills that sat by the shores of the lake. Lake Windermere was busy with its usual variety of boats, from the large steamers that plough up and down its ten-mile length, to yachts, canoes and small rowing boats like the *Curlew*.

Tom and Harry spent most weekends at their local water-sports centre, and their skills were being put to good use today. They had to be especially careful to keep well clear of the large steamers; if they got too close the ship's captain wouldn't see them. Rowing slowly, weaving between larger moored boats, they headed down the lake on their planned circuit of Belle Isle.

'I'll row with the flow of the lake first,' said Harry.

Later, as he turned against the flow, rowing up the other side of Belle Isle, he had found his steady rowing technique. Being a tall and well-built boy he had good control of the little boat. He wore a cap to control his wild, wavy hair, so he could see where he was going.

After completing the circuit of Belle Isle they decided to land on one of the smaller islands, and make it their own, just for a few hours. So they carefully landed the *Curlew* on the small pebble shore and secured it with the rope to a large boulder.

'What's this island called?' said Tom, as he chomped on a piece of flapjack.

'Dunno,' said Harry, 'I'll have a look at the map.'

Tom hurled a stone into the lake; *plunk* – it went straight down.

'Not one bounce!' sniggered Harry.

'I wasn't trying to skim! You have a go and we can have a contest.'

But Harry, still looking at the map, had just realised

he hadn't marked on the landing place where they had set up camp.

'You carry on,' Harry replied, 'I'll just be a minute.' His mind wasn't really on the skimming but half-heartedly he joined in eventually. Tom won the contest with five bounces on his last throw.

As they walked around the edge of the island, they realised they were the only ones on it, and made their way up to the rocks at the very top that gave them an all-round view. They looked with delight at the beautiful mountains, and recognised what's called the Fairfield Horseshoe range, which curls around the top of the lake. They couldn't see some parts of the lake, as they were hidden by Belle Isle.

Tom wandered off as Harry peered through the binoculars, trying to spot where they had put up the tent. All of a sudden, he heard a huge **splash**, followed by a frenzied fluttering and quacking. He quickly bounded down towards the commotion. Tom, coughing and spluttering, came crawling out of the lake, drenched.

'What on earth is going on?' yelled Harry.

'I've just rescued some ducklings!' gasped Tom. 'They were stuck. I was trying to reach them and fell in, I couldn't see the edge of the lake under all the leaves and brambles!'

Looking behind Tom, Harry saw a tangle of brambles and the branches of a fallen tree sprawling into the lake. In the clear water, a mother duck and a line of tiny ducklings were paddling away, happy to be back together again. A good deed done, Tom dried himself off on the pebble beach, in the warmth of the setting sun.

Chapter Two

After untying the *Curlew*, and with another careful launch, Tom started rowing back towards the shore. Tom was almost as tall as Harry, and although he was slimmer than his brother, he was strong for his size, and his strength and the practice he had done at weekends helped him manage the boat. Harry, still annoyed with himself for not marking the exact landing place on the map, was using his binoculars, trying to spot any landmarks he might recognise near to the camp. It was difficult; a lot of the areas around the lake looked the same. It was dusk, and the air was becoming misty as they stopped at the first bay that looked like it could have been theirs.

'I think you should stop rowing now,' said Harry. Tom was surprised, as he thought Harry sounded a bit worried.

'Why?' asked Tom, 'We aren't near the shore yet ... are we lost?'

'I'm still looking!' snapped Harry. 'Be quiet while I concentrate.'

Tom began to get a bit chilly now that he wasn't rowing any more, and a shiver ran down his back. He wanted to say 'I wish Dad was here', but chose not to, in case Harry snapped at him again.

As they both looked towards the shore an odd stillness seemed to creep around them. The *Curlew* did not move at all in the still lake. There was only the sound of water dripping from the oars and the flapping sails of the distant boats. The boys felt quite alone in the silence, and as the mist became thicker they started to become afraid that they would never find their camp.

Suddenly they heard an eerie, whispering voice.

'This is not your bay! Don't land here!'

'Shush Tom!' said Harry. 'I said I'm trying to concentrate!'

'I never spoke!' insisted Tom.

'This is not the bay! Don't land here!' They heard the strangely distant but clear voice again.

'Who is that?' asked Tom, starting to feel a little bit afraid.

'Look, up there, it's someone on the hill!' whispered Harry.

'Row further down the lake ... ' instructed the haunting voice.

Trying to peer through the mist, the boys could see the outline of a white, mysterious figure in a clearing of the woods.

'Whoever it is,' said Harry, ' I think we should keep on rowing. This is creepy, and our camp clearly isn't here. I'll keep looking out.'

As Tom rowed across to the next small bay, Harry was sure they couldn't be far off the landing place.

They heard the ghostly figure speak again. It seemed nearer now.

'Stop … this is where you should land.'

They both looked upwards. 'He's moved along the hill!' said Tom.

'Woah!' shouted Harry, beaming with relief. 'He's exactly above where we need to land; I think I can make out our tent! Row in Tom!'

As Tom pulled hard on one of the oars, the *Curlew* swung around towards the shore. He rowed into the bay and they lost sight of the pale figure, but that didn't matter, they were almost in the landing place. After pulling the boat ashore, they quickly tied it up and they were soon back at the camp.

'How weird was that?' exclaimed Harry, confused by what had happened. After all, they hadn't been able to see this figure clearly, only a snow-white glowing shape through the mist. They wondered how anyone could know who they were from up there in the woods, and where they needed to land.

'Only Dad knows where we tied the boat up. Was it him trying to help us, do you think?' said Tom.

'I doubt it,' said Harry. 'Dad would have been down here by the lake if he thought we were lost, not up in the woods. Anyway, come on, let's get the fire going, I'm starving.'

Both boys were now ravenous as it was way past dinnertime, and all talk of the mysterious helper stopped as they got busy making a hot meal. Harry made a ring of stones for a fireplace while Tom collected twigs and small broken branches to burn. Sausages, eggs and bacon sizzled in the frying pan, while jacket potatoes roasted in the fire.

As they sat round the campfire devouring their delicious supper, washing it down with home-made lemonade, they began to wonder again: who *was* it that had guided them home?

'Let's row out to our island again in the morning,'

suggested Harry. 'We can have a good look across to the hills with the binoculars. We might be able to spot a house or farm where someone lives.'

'Yeah,' Tom agreed, 'it would be great to find out who helped us and thank them.' With a plan now decided for tomorrow, they eventually got into their sleeping bags and drifted off into a deep sleep.

The morning sun lit up the tent, waking them early. Sorting their dreams out from reality, they both recalled yesterday's weird events and the plans they had made for the morning. After breakfast they headed for the shore and untied the boat. And before Tom had a chance to remind him, Harry immediately marked the landing place for the camp on the map. They rowed carefully through all the other boats and headed towards their island.

They tied the *Curlew* to the boulder and made their way to the craggy top. They both scanned the woods of Claife Heights above their camp with binoculars, trying to find some clue about yesterday's bizarre encounter. They could not see any buildings and the woodland was so thick it was difficult to find a place where someone could have actually seen the shoreline from the woods. They returned to their boat, still without any explanation of last night's helpful haunting visitor.

They rowed the *Curlew* back to the shore and this time, after using the map to set the compass direction, headed straight to their landing place. They were at the camp well before nightfall and Tom was about to light the campfire. But yesterday's events were still on Harry's mind.

'Tom, do you fancy going for a snoop round the ferry house?' he asked. 'There may be a ranger based there, and we can ask him about yesterday.'

'Will we get to ride on the ferry?' Tom answered with another question.

'I don't see why not, if it's still running! We'd have time to sail both ways, too, if we're quick.'

Chapter Three

Off they went at a run. After a quick check on the time the last ferry returned, they were soon on board for a trip across the lake. As the ferry made its short journey, they looked up towards Claife Heights and the woods above their camp. Harry was thinking of asking a member of the crew about the strange ghostly figure and the voice they had heard. But now, in broad daylight, it all sounded rather foolish. Still, they had to find *something* out.

'Excuse me,' he said to the friendliest-looking man of the crew, 'are there any ranger patrols to help a boat that's in trouble?'

'No need to worry about us,' the friendly face said, 'we aren't thinking of sinking today!'

Tom cut in on Harry's conversation and came straight to the point.

'Are there any ghosts around here?' he blurted out, and continued before the crewman could answer. 'Because last night we got lost on our boat and we heard a voice. Someone or something shouted to us from up there,' he added, pointing to the woods.

The crewman smiled. 'Ghosts?' he chuckled. 'Voices? Well, I don't know. There's only a ranger on the lake, not up in the hills.' After a moment's thought he added, 'Look, Old Ben is calling in to see us later. If anyone knows about voices and ghosts around here, it'll be Ben. He ran this ferry for forty years. He's here for our reunion tonight and he likes a good tale. Are you coming back with us, because this is the last crossing?'

'Yes,' said Tom. 'We only came on the ferry to find

out about the voice, and we want to thank whoever it may be.'

'Well then,' the friendly crewman said, 'you can come to the ferry house and ask Old Ben for yourself.'

When they returned across the lake, the crewman took them inside the ferry house, and in the corner sat Ben the old ferryman.

'Hello Ben,' he said, 'I've brought these youngsters here to see you. They have a bit of a ghostly tale to ask you about.'

Old Ben, stroking his bushy beard, looked a bit puzzled, but without hesitation Harry told him the full story.

'Well I never,' Ben said. 'I've heard some tales in my time but I think you children have topped the lot!'

'It's not a tale!' Tom exclaimed.

'Shush,' said Harry, 'don't be cheeky.'

'Nay,' said Old Ben, 'I'm not saying the story's not true, but listen up while I tell you two a tale of my own. Years ago – nay hundreds of years ago – when this ferry was no more than a big rowing boat, people said there was a ghost about then. "The Crier", they called him. He used to keep on calling on the ferryman, and every time he rowed across lake to pick up what he thought was going to be some passengers, there was nobody there. Now, this had gone on for many a week. Ferryman had had just about enough of it. Like I said, his boat didn't have any motor; he had to row across. So off to the church he went to see the priest, and *he* had an idea who it was. He remembered a few years earlier there had been a monk, who'd fallen in love with a nun. Now, this isn't allowed, monks and nuns must never marry. Anyway, the monk died of a broken heart, so they say, and the old priest reckoned the monk's spirit was still looking for his beloved nun. So the priest did what they had to do, and laid the monk's spirit to rest with a bible, candle and holy words – he banished it forever. Or that's what they thought.'

Tom and Harry sat there with wide eyes and

mouths open. Neither of them knew what to say.

Old Ben continued. 'Now then, from what you lads say, it looks like The Crier's back. But it seems he's doing good deeds these days if he guided you home. Well I never, not many round here even believed in the tale!'

'Well we certainly do,' said Harry recovering his speech, with Tom nodding in agreement.

'Well, well,' said Ben. 'We won't be the only ones. Those map-making people know about him too. I don't think they put many ghosts on their maps but next time you look, you'll find The Crier marked up in those woods.'

'Now then,' said Ben, turning to the crewman, 'where are we going for this here reunion? I'm ready for a drink after all this spooky talk.'

It was getting late, so the boys thanked Old Ben and the crewman and made their way back to camp, chattering nonstop about Ben's tale and The Crier. With the night closing in, they decided to wait until morning to have a proper look at the map. After their supper, the fire was put out and they were soon snug in their sleeping bags inside the tent. They slept soundly again, tired from the excitement of the day.

It was cloudy next morning and the sun didn't wake them, so it had to be a quick breakfast before taking the tent down, clearing out the fireplace and having a big clean up. When they had finished, no one would have known they had ever been there. They wanted to come again next year so they made sure everything was left just right.

When their parents arrived, Harry could hardly get a word in as Tom told the story without pausing for breath. Harry's mum and dad found the story hard to believe, that is, until they heard the old ferryman's tale of The Crier.

While Tom was still gabbling on, Harry unfolded the map. He just hoped Old Ben was right, but he still had some doubt that the name of the ghost would be marked on a modern map. The boys' dad came across to where Harry had flattened out the map. But there it was, marked in the woods, on the map, exactly like Old Ben had explained.

'Look! It *is* here!' cried Harry, pointing at the map. 'The Crier of Claife!'

TRAPPED IN MOONSHINE MINE

What is moonshine?

In the nineteenth century, mining was a big industry in the English Lake District. Slate, copper, lead and even silver were dug out from mines deep under the mountains of Helvellyn, Coniston Old Man and Honister Crag. The business made a lot of money, but the work was hard and never-ending. Some men were known to steal nuggets of the goods to increase their very small wages. Other men went about their own secret activities, such as making illegal whisky, which is called 'moonshine', with their hidden, home-made equipment. Using the mine ponies they would smuggle the moonshine out of the mines through abandoned tunnels. This is where our story begins.

Chapter One

(Eastern Lake District, 1864)

It was to be a great weekend for moving the moonshine over the mountain. George Braithwaite had done most of the heavy preparation work. He'd got everything ready with the ponies and removed the boulders from the end of the tunnel in the next valley, but his partner had vanished again. George had decided that his dodgy partnership with Bill Pattinson would soon have to end.

After moving the moonshine all by himself and over the mountain to the next cave, George returned to the mine. He took all his secret equipment apart and hid it down a side tunnel.

When he met his partner Bill a few days later for their shift in the lead mine, he heard the same old story. Bill's wife had been down with sickness and he had had to look after the children again. George knew this was another lie. The mine blacksmith had already told him he'd seen Bill in the pub on Sunday!

After their proper work in the daytime, they'd usually meet up in the evening for their illegal work. Bill was in their secret tunnel first.

'Some guards must have stolen our equipment!' he said.

'Aye,' George scoffed. 'And how am *I* to know it wasn't *you*?!'

'I told you George, my wife has gone down sick again, and I had to look after the children.'

'Was that after you met Lanty and before you went to the pub?'

'What are you on about George, I've never heard

of someone called Lanty?'

'You know who I mean. Lancelot then, or whatever he calls himself.'

'Oh you mean *him*, who still uses pigs' bladders to carry his moonshine around in?'

'So you *do* know him then,' said George, rolling his eyes.

'Remember it was me who got you all those nice bottles,' said Bill, ignoring George's comment. 'Nobody wants Lanty Slee's moonshine any more, not in those horrible pigs' bladders, it's our stuff they want.'

'Ah, Lanty *Slee* is it now? Thought you'd never heard of him?'

Bill knew he had been rumbled. He had called in to see Lanty Slee, but only about some money he was owed. He wanted to get his money back before Slee was jailed. Rumour had it that this time Slee was in for a hefty sentence after he'd tried to sell his moonshine to some undercover policemen. Even though he didn't work with Slee any more, it was the last chance Bill had to get the money he was due. However much he tried to explain this to him, because of his previous lies George didn't believe that Bill had stopped working with Lanty Slee.

After their last load of moonshine was smuggled out, making them quite a lot of money, George ended his partnership with Bill. The tunnel wasn't going to be of much use anyway. A shooting lodge was going to be built close to the tunnel exit in the next valley. Although the lodge owners were unaware of the tunnel, it would be too risky to use again. Determined to start making the moonshine elsewhere, George pulled the last two props out of the tunnel, and collapsed the entrance, making sure it could never be used again – by Bill or anyone else.

Chapter Two

(Eastern Lake District, 150 years later)

This year Harry and Tom Daly and their parents were staying in a holiday cottage in Patterdale. Mr Daly's work friend had let them use it for a number of years now, and the family knew the area well.

Their favourite walk of all was the climb up Helvellyn and along the knife-edge ridge route known as Striding Edge. The walk was always planned for a fine day. It was a sunny morning, the first day of their holiday, as they made their way up from the valley. With dry rocks and not a breath of wind, all four of them crossed the edge in high spirits; even Tom was confident enough to stride over the gap in the rocky hilltop. Their father always said this was the stride that the edge was named after. They avoided the edges on their return and found it interesting to go along a different path, through some old mine workings. Mr Daly explained details of the mines that were last used back in 1962. However, Tom was more interested in using his new binoculars to watch the buzzards in a mid-air battle with the crows. He was so engrossed that his mother had to shout more than once for him to catch up with them.

He only realised when they arrived back at the cottage that he'd left the binoculars behind. He turned around as they reached the cottage gate, saying, 'I'll have to go back to the mine I've left my bi … '

'You're not going back up there tonight Tom,' interrupted his mother. 'We're going to have supper and you won't have time before it goes dark.'

'Oh Mum, it's raining now, they're new and they'll

get wet! I'll take a torch!'

'You and Harry can go together in the morning,' she said. 'You really should be more careful – I don't know how you do it!'

Tom hardly slept that night and was up early to wake Harry.

'Come on Harry, we can get up to the old mine before breakfast.'

Harry was having none of it. 'You're not getting me in trouble! We can't go until everyone's up and had breakfast. Anyway I'm still tired.' Harry was right, as their mother insisted on breakfast.

'Dad and I will be doing some shopping,' their mum said, 'so I've put some sandwiches together for you both. If you want a chocolate bar, call in at the shop.'

'Thanks!' said Harry, as he popped them in his rucksack.

They called in at the shop and Mr Cruickshank was his usual nosy self.

'Oh, you two are back again, what are you up to today?'

'Just walking,' said Harry.

Tom was about to tell Mr Cruickshank about the binoculars. 'Oww!' he said, as Harry stood on his toe.

'Keep out of the old mine area, it's very dangerous round there,' said the shopkeeper. 'It's no place for boys!'

Eventually he passed Harry his change and said goodbye with his usual scowl.

'Come on Tom,' said Harry, before he had chance to speak about where they were going.

The boys soon arrived at the mine but the binoculars weren't where Tom had expected to see them. It was Harry who spotted something else that was out of place, the cover for one of the old mine shafts. He remembered seeing it the day before in its proper position, covering the opening into the mine. It was now wide open. By the cover was a sign and Harry read it aloud.

When he looked round Tom was nowhere to be seen. Harry looked towards the shaft and spotted the top of his head disappearing down it.

'Tom, what on earth are you playing at? Get out of there *now*!' he shouted.

'It's okay, there's a light on down here!'

'I don't care Tom, get out now!' demanded Harry. He could no longer see Tom, so followed him down the shaft ladder and into the tunnel.

'Come on Tom, we shouldn't be here,' he whispered.

As the lights were on in the tunnel, Harry instinctively sensed they weren't alone.

'But what about my bino ... '

'Shush!' snapped Harry. 'Never mind them, come on back up the ladder.' He moved further into the tunnel after him.

'They're not going to be in here, are they?' continued Harry.

'Okay,' sighed Tom, 'keep your hair on, I'm coming.'

As they turned round, they heard men's voices coming from a side tunnel they hadn't noticed. Dashing back into the shadows, they watched two men disappear up the ladder of the shaft. The tunnel lights suddenly went out and now there was only a glimmer of light coming from the shaft opening. They heard a dull thud and the screech of metal on metal as the men replaced and locked the cover into position. Harry and Tom were trapped. The tunnel was now completely dark.

Chapter Three

'Look what's happened now!' shouted Harry. 'How could you be so stupid?'

He felt a wave of panic inside him, but he needed to remain calm. However foolish Tom had been, Harry knew he had to stay strong. Tom tried to stifle his sobs. 'I … I didn't know … any … anybody was down … h … here,' he spluttered.

In any other situation Harry would have teased his younger brother, but he said, 'Lucky I didn't leave the rucky up there,' as he rooted in the rucksack for his torch. 'I'll have a look at that cover and see if I can push it off. Don't worry Tom, we'll soon be out of here,' he continued, trying to make light of their desperate situation.

He climbed to the top of the vertical ladder and pushed with all his might. He was a strong teenager with muscular arms from years of rowing, but he could not shift the heavy metal cover. He gave up, realising it must be locked from the outside.

Telling Tom to stay where he was, he explored the side tunnel where the men had come from. He had only entered a few feet when the beam of the torch flashed a reflection. As Harry got closer to the glint he saw bottles neatly stacked in crates. Further down the tunnel he spotted a contraption, like a miniature version of the equipment he once saw at a Speyside whisky distillery while on holiday in the Scottish Highlands. Bemused by his find he picked up a bottle from a crate.

'Angel's Drop', he read from the label. It was an unusual place, he thought, for whisky to be stored, and he put the bottle in his rucksack to show his father. Harry didn't want to waste any more time there; they needed to get out and he made his way back to Tom.

'We can't get out through that cover, it's solid. And the side tunnel is a dead end,' said Harry.

'There must be a way out!' insisted Tom desperately. He had now recovered from the initial shock and sudden darkness.

'Listen,' continued Harry, 'we haven't got many options. We can either wait until the men come back, but who knows when that will be. Or … '

'We can try the other end of this tunnel,' interrupted Tom.

'It may be the best idea after what I've just seen.'

'Why, what have you seen?'

Harry told Tom about the equipment and bottles of whisky. 'Somehow I don't think those men are going to be pleased to see us,' he added.

'Wow!' said Tom, and then another idea came to him, which would have been more obvious to them both if it weren't for the shock of being trapped. 'Did you try your mobile?' he asked.

'Good idea but I don't think I'll get a signal down here.'

'Go up the ladder and try it near the cover,' suggested Tom.

Harry tried his mobile phone by the cover but the signal kept disappearing as he tried to ring his mother's phone. Then he hit on a better idea – he tapped out a text message:

Mum sorry 2 worry u, me and T r ok but trapped in the mine under the opening we saw ydy. Long story but we r trying 2 find another way out. H xx

He pressed the send button but still the signal wasn't strong enough. He put the phone in his pocket and came back down the ladder into the tunnel.

'No luck, Tom. Come on, let's see if there's another way out down this main tunnel.' They scrambled as fast as they dare with only the torchlight to show the way. Edging round ankle-deep puddles became impossible as they travelled further into the mountain. The tunnel walls narrowed, and soon murky water covered the ground completely. In places, rockfall debris from the tunnel roof and walls filled the puddles. This helped progress but with the constant dripping of water both boys feared they might get trapped in the tunnel by a flood or maybe by rockfall. At one point Tom tripped over an old rotten prop that was hidden in the water but he jumped up and kept going, ignoring the shock of the ice-cold water that soaked through to his skin. The tunnel became so narrow they found themselves shuffling sideways and then came to a sudden halt. There was another huge roof fall in front of them, with no way around it. To their horror the tunnel had come to an abrupt end.

'Best get back to the other end again,' said Tom. 'That's where Mum and Dad will be looking, if they ever get your text message.'

Harry took the phone out of his pocket and read the screen, '*Message not sent – do you want to try again?*' So he hit the OK button.

They waited a moment and then Harry said, 'The message isn't going, we've got to keep looking for a way out.' Trying to keep Tom's spirits up, he continued. 'Look it's only a few minutes since we passed another tunnel junction; let's just see what there is down there.' They returned to the junction and as they entered the side tunnel they saw a crate of old bottles covered in dust.

'They must have been here years,' said Tom.

Behind another pile of rubble Harry could make out what looked like some more old whisky-making equipment.

'Look at this Tom, it's ancient. It's just like the contraption I saw in the other tunnel, but it's been here years.'

A little further on there was another tunnel collapse, this time from a side wall. On closer inspection with the torch they noticed some building stone amongst the debris. The wall had been patched up with wooden boards, some of which were rotten. Tom took a swing with his boot and the boards gave way.

'Woah!' shouted Harry. 'We don't want another rockfall!'

'But it's hollow behind,' said Tom, as he bent down and pulled off another section of the rotten timber and dragged his foot out. He continued to pull more off until he could squeeze his head through the jagged hole. 'It's a hut of some sort. There must be windows – it's bright and light!' he said as he manoeuvred his head back out of the hole.

'Okay,' said Harry, 'if we take it easy, let's see if we can make the hole big enough for us to get through.'

Both boys carefully tore at the small opening. As they got more confident they kicked pieces through using the kung fu technique that was usually practised on each other. Eventually, Tom first and then Harry emerged into a large climbers' hut.

Chapter Four

Mr and Mrs Daly were enjoying lunch on the top floor of their favourite hikers' shop in Keswick. They were absorbed with the views towards Grisedale Pike, thinking that this must be the most fantastic view from a town centre cafe in England. The text alert tone on Mrs Daly's mobile phone broke their daydream.

'It's the boys!' she shrieked, silencing the rest of the cafe. 'They're trapped down that awful mine!' Turning pale she passed the phone to her husband.

He immediately dialled 999 and explained exactly the location of the disused mining area where their sons were trapped. Half an hour later they were driving up the mine road in Glenridding. The area close to the converted mine buildings was already crowded with vehicles – mountain rescue, police cars and national park Land Rovers. Mr Daly nearly missed the urgently arranged control point, but just managed to stop when he saw the police officer.

'Sorry there's no access beyond this point today sir, you'll have to turn round,' the police officer instructed.

'We phoned earlier, we're Mr and Mrs Daly, the parents of the boys in the mine – Harry and Thomas!'

At that the policeman guided them to park behind a mountain rescue vehicle. 'Please wait here, I'll radio the inspector.'

From where they had parked, Mr and Mrs Daly could see all the activity round the tunnel opening with the entrance cover now removed again.

Meanwhile, the boys sat down on a bench, in what was now a climbers' hut. There was enough light for them to see even though the windows were boarded over. With their relief at being out of the tunnel they now began to feel hungry. Harry put the torch back in the rucksack and brought out the picnic. They regained some calmness while wolfing down the sandwiches.

Harry tried the door of the hut but it was locked tight. 'We might be able to get this lock off, Tom,' he said. 'Have you got that scout knife of yours?'

Tom passed Harry his knife. 'Here, if you know what you're looking for.'

Harry pulled out several of the gadgets until he found just the screwdriver he needed.

'Great, I'll have a go with this.' After a painstaking few minutes he managed to loosen and remove the rusty screws and yanked the lock from the door frame. He pulled the door open and they were out in the fresh air at last.

The hut was located right by a footpath, but after being in the mine tunnels they were completely disorientated, and they covered their eyes as they were dazzled from the daylight.

As they became accustomed to the brightness, Harry looked both ways on the path. One way led up to a mountain track and the other down, along the side of the valley.

'Come on, this way,' he said, 'we've got to go down.' As they walked, the area became more familiar to them.

'Look up there Harry, I'm sure that's the path up to the edge,' said Tom, pointing out the track towards the renowned Hole in the Wall. 'We were walking up there only yesterday. That means we must be in Grisedale, walking towards Lanty's Tarn. By the way, has your text message sent yet?'

'Oh no! I forgot all about that!' Harry reached for his phone. 'Yeah, it must have sent as we came out of the mine.' He noticed a new inbox message:

On our way, we have phoned the police don't do anything else foolish, the rescue services will be there before us – Mum xx

'Just tell Mum we're okay,' said Tom. 'Say sorry, but I bet we're in for it when we see them … '

'I can't, the battery's flat, it's just cut out altogether,' grumbled Harry.

They heard sirens, which seemed to be coming from the next valley. Harry and Tom stared at each other, mouths open, but speechless. Quickening their pace it wasn't long before they were walking alongside Lanty's Tarn. Then instead of heading back to Glenridding they took the path that led towards the mine road. They were soon jogging up the road towards the police control point.

'That looks like our car! Is that Dad talking to a policeman?!' cried Tom.

Both boys began shrieking. 'Muuuumm! Daaaadd!'

Mrs Daly looked round and ran down the road to meet them. She grabbed both boys and hugged them together. Neither Harry nor Tom wanted to let her go, as Mr Daly walked towards them, shaking his head.

Chapter Five

Following the initial relief all round, there were still a lot of questions to be answered. And not just to their parents; the police wanted answers too.

'How did you manage to get the mineshaft cover off?'

Harry stayed calm as he explained again. 'It was already off,' he said, glancing across to his father and back again to the inspector.

'Look lads, no one wants to give you a lecture,' said the inspector. 'We're all just glad you're out, but we do need to know how you got that cover off.'

'It must have been the men, Harry,' said Tom, trying to help. 'Remember they came out of that side tunnel, where you saw the crates of whisky, near the shaft.'

'Tom! They're not bothered about that,' interrupted Harry.

'Just a minute, we found that old equipment and the bottles near the climbing lodge end,' said the inspector. 'They must have been there since Lanty Slee's time. But what's all this about men and bottles in a side tunnel near the shaft entrance? Come on lad,' said the inspector to Harry, 'if you know anything else you need to tell us.'

Harry then opened his rucksack and brought out a shiny new bottle of the Angel's Drop.

'I only took it to show Dad,' he said as he passed it to the inspector. 'I'll pay for it.'

'What on earth have you got here?' The inspector read out the label on the bottle: '*Angel's Drop the finest malt whisky aged 10 years in oak casks.*' 'I can hardly believe this,' said the inspector. 'Are you up here for a

ANGEL'S DROP
THE FINEST MALT WHISKY
AGED
10
YEARS
IN OAK CASKS

few more days, Mr Daly? We need your lads to show us exactly where this came from.'

'Sorry Dad, what's going to happen to us?' Harry sniffled.

'Happen to you, lad? You're probably going to get a nice big reward,' said the inspector. 'We've been looking for this gang of modern-day moonshiners for years!'

'They sell bottles just like this in the village shop,' said Mrs Daly. 'This one must have been stolen from there.'

'Not quite,' said the inspector. 'These have been

supplied to Mr Cruickshank's shop by his crooked friends. We've been keeping an eye on Cruickshank for some time now.'

The following day the mine was opened up again and Harry and Tom showed the police down to the side tunnel. The crates of Angel's Drop and the equipment were exactly as Harry found them. The boys wanted to go further into the tunnel to show Dad the old equipment and bottles, but they were told that access to that part of the mine was unsafe as the tunnel was completely flooded.

Back in the village as they made their way to the cottage the boys could see more police action outside the village shop. Mr Cruickshank still managed one of his trademark scowls at the boys as he was led out handcuffed to a police officer.

Harry and Tom received two letters in the weeks following their eventful holiday. The first was an invitation to an award ceremony from the chief constable of Cumbria. They were to be presented with a 'substantial' reward and a medal of commendation each. This was in recognition of their help with the detention of four men arrested and now in custody awaiting trial for smuggling and avoiding paying their taxes. The second letter was from a Lake District National Park archaeologist. She advised them that they had indeed made a very interesting discovery of the old equipment and bottles. It was proof that illicit liquor was made and smuggled from the mining site in the nineteenth century with no previous records of it.

They also received a copy of the *Westmorland Gazette* with a full report under the headline: 'Legend of Lanty Slee lives on. Present-day bootleggers jailed!'

THE FIERY
FARMER

DOG OWNERS
DUE TO SEVERAL INCIDENTS
PLEASE KEEP YOUR DOGS
ON LEADS
ANY DOGS SEEN CHASING SHEEP
COULD BE SHOT!

It was the first time Elle had seen the new bright red sign. 'Hold Daisy will you Dec, while I open the gate,' she said, passing her brother the dog's lead. But as Declan opened his hand to take it, he dropped the other dog's lead and Tara ran off up the hillside.

It was a lovely sunny day, just the sort everyone hopes for on the first day of a holiday in the Lake District. Shorts and light-coloured T-shirts were the order of the day, but of course stout walking boots were always required on this hill – there always seemed to be boggy areas whatever the weather. Elle was pleased that they were out on the hills with the dogs on their own for the first time. She knew the routes up this hill very well, but this wasn't a good start to the walk. Dad had said it would be a good idea for them to go out while he and Mum unpacked for their week's holiday in the caravan. Mum wasn't too sure because the dogs – a pair of springer spaniels – were full of beans and always causing chaos, especially Tara. However, she thought with Elle now twelve and Declan ten they should be okay if they kept the dogs on their leads.

At first Elle was quite relaxed about it, as Tara always came back as quick as she ran off. But this time she ran off the path and continued out of sight round the curve of the hill. Elle told Declan to keep a tight hold of Daisy while she ran after Tara. Typical, thought Elle, how could this happen on their first hill walk without Mum and Dad? She stopped and shouted a while, but knew she would have to get back to her brother.

'We'll have to carry on,' she said, 'and maybe Tara will pick up our scent and come back to us on the way up.'

'But what about that sign?' said Declan. 'If the farmer sees Tara first he might shoot her!'

'Well hopefully she won't be chasing the sheep!' They carried on with Daisy whimpering, obviously fretting for Tara.

The hill began to level out before the last rise to the summit, and they climbed on to a nearby crag that gave them a good all-round view. Usually they only had eyes for the great bulk of Skiddaw – on full view now with a clear summit – or Bassenthwaite Lake, shimmering in the sunshine with all the mountains beyond. Normally they'd be competing to name them. Today all eyes were towards the ground. They scanned the area below and could see all the way back to the caravan site, the road, the lane and the gate where they'd lost Tara. Behind them, where they had just been walking, were great masses of heather. Surely, thought Elle, Tara may dart in and out of the undergrowth but wouldn't settle there. There was no sign of her anywhere. Daisy was straining on her lead every direction they turned.

'Let her off the lead,' said Declan, 'she may pick up a scent.'

'Oh yeah good idea,' Elle replied, scoffing, 'then we can lose them both!'

'Okay you think of something then, clever clogs!'

'Alright, let's just get to the top first,' she said, 'then if we can't find her there we will have to think of something else.'

To add to their panic they heard the sudden *crack* of gunfire ring through the hills. The horrible silence that followed was disturbed by a flock of crows, noisily cawing, flying up from the trees below.

'What if that was the farmer shooting at Tara?'

cried Declan, desperately looking around him.

'Shut up Declan, don't even think of it,' snapped Elle, 'we've got to keep moving and find her quick!'

They reached the cairn on the stony hilltop, but there was still no sign of the little dog.

'Right, now what?' asked Declan.

'Shush,' said Elle, 'I can hear something … '

'What, Tara?' said Declan, squinting around the hillside.

'No listen, it's the farmer on his quad bike. I can see him; he'll be up on the level patch soon. Hold on tight to Daisy!' Elle shouted, as she ran back down towards the farmer.

Farmer Gilkes had had a busy morning looking for a lost cow. Now he saw a young girl running down the hill waving her arms about. The last thing he wanted was to deal with another lost or injured hillwalker. As Elle drew closer he stopped the quad bike. Within seconds she was with the farmer, trying to speak but too breathless to get the words out.

'Hold on lass, catch your breath!' said Bill Gilkes, as he lifted his cap up and ruffled his greying hair.

'We've lost our dog, Tara,' she managed to say, just as she spotted the farmer's gun in a box on the quad bike.

'I haven't seen any dog,' the farmer said, 'but if she's worrying my sheep she'll be in trouble.'

'We heard the gunfire, please don't shoot Tara,' begged Elle, looking straight at the gruff old farmer.

'That wily fox dodged the shot again,' said the farmer. 'I'll have him next time.'

'Oh! A fox … ' sighed Elle, with huge relief.

'I'm too busy to bother about a dog – I'm looking for a cow that's got lost somewhere,' said the farmer. 'You find her quick and get her back on that lead.' And with that, he fired up the quad bike and drove off.

Elle made her way back up to Declan, who was still on the hilltop.

'It was a fox', she said, 'the farmer shot at a fox.'

'What about Tara?' he asked.

'It's no good,' she said, 'he hasn't seen her. But we need to find her quick, he didn't seem too pleased.'

'Daisy's been pulling hard to go down there,' Declan said, pointing down the other side of the hill. 'All I can hear is that noisy cow mooing.'

'Come on then,' said Elle, 'keep her on the lead but let's follow her.'

They set off bounding down the hill, Declan being dragged by Daisy. As they rounded a small copse they caught sight of Tara springing about and yelping down into a hole.

'Hurray!' shrieked Elle. 'There you are, you naughty dog! Nice one Daisy.'

'I hope she hasn't killed a sheep … ' said Declan.

They soon reached Tara, but were amazed to see not a sheep in the hole, but a cow, 'mooooing,' up towards the sky.

'Quick, get her back on the lead Dec. It looks like the cow's trapped,' said Elle seriously. 'The farmer said he was looking for a lost cow.'

Then they heard the quad bike again and tried to attract the farmer's attention, but he seemed to be ignoring them. This time Elle held on to both dogs and Declan set off at a run after the farmer, who eventually pulled up.

'I haven't got time to be bothered with you kids all day, I told that lass I'm looking for a cow.'

'We know where your cow is!' yelled Declan above the noise of the quad bike. The farmer immediately switched the engine off.

'Where?' he asked abruptly.

'Over there,' Declan pointed towards Elle and the dogs.

'I don't see any beasts,' replied the farmer gruffly.

'There is, honest, it's in a hollow.'

'If you kids are messing me about I'll have you off this hill in no time,' said the farmer. He then got off his quad bike and walked down the hillside. Declan ran down, and was quick to pick Tara up; he saw the farmer's gun and remembered the sign they'd seen that morning. Tara was still whimpering towards the hole in the ground with the trapped animal.

'Well I never,' the farmer said, 'who'd have thought it? Did your mongrel find my beast?'

'She's called Tara,' said Elle.

'Aye, Tara, she's done a good job then, worthy of a job on my farm.'

'How will you get it out?' asked Declan.

'If you kids aren't dashing off you could help. I'm going to strap this tarpaulin sheet around her middle and then I'll have to pull her out with the quad.'

They watched, fascinated as he worked the tarpaulin sheet under the cow. He wasn't a big man but was obviously very strong. Farmer Gilkes then rode the quad bike closer to the cow as Elle dragged the rope over for the farmer to attach to the tow bar.

'Can you watch her as she comes out? Mind her legs don't get trapped! Don't be frightened she won't bite,' said the farmer.

Elle and Declan weren't afraid, they were used to

working with animals at the farm where Elle's horse was stabled. As the farmer slowly moved the quad bike, Declan and Elle pushed and shoved for all they were worth. The dogs encouraged with non-stop barking and the cow's thunderous mooing all added to what must have looked like such a bizarre scene. Eventually she emerged with no harm done and ambled off to join the rest of the herd further down the hillside. They recovered their composure and looked down into the circular hole – about two metres wide and over one metre deep with stone-lined sides.

'Look at that,' said Declan, 'a man-made hole.' 'Is it the top of an old mineshaft?' asked Elle.

'No, it's an old shooting butt,' explained the farmer. 'I thought I'd filled them all in. They're not used any more. I must have missed this one,' said the farmer.

He looked on at his group of helpers, who were covered from head to toe in mud.

'I think I owe you children! Are you staying nearby?' he asked.

'Yes we're at the caravan park, we've only just arrived,' said Elle.

'Well you'd better come to the farmhouse and get cleaned up before you go back.'

Farmer Gilkes put the gun away in the rifle case and made room for them all to climb on to the quad bike. Moving slowly down towards the big white farmhouse, Elle and Declan could see the farmer's wife in the distance pegging out the washing. As the quad bike drew nearer she looked round, astonished to see the farmer's passengers.

'What in the world … ' said the surprised farmer's wife, but before she could finish, the farmer had switched off the engine and explained how the children had helped find and rescue the cow.

'Your mum and dad won't thank us for getting you in such a state!' she said. So she brought them into the big farmhouse kitchen and helped to clean them up.

'We saw the new sign,' said Declan, ' and we're just glad he didn't shoot Tara.'

'Now did you hear that?' said the kind lady to her husband. 'I told you I didn't like that sign! I think you can do these children a favour now and change it. Threatening to shoot dogs? Goodness me!'

'Aye you're right, the sign will be changed before their holiday's over. And next year,' he said to the children, 'when you're up here for your holiday you can stay in our holiday cottage for a week free of charge.'

Mrs Gilkes then explained to the children that her husband had only ever carried the gun to shoot foxes since the hunting ban a few years before. She packed a box with eggs, milk and butter and gave the children a letter for their mum and dad with the offer of a week's stay in the holiday cottage. She said it was the least they could do. And true to his word the farmer changed the sign.

Before their holiday ended all the family did the hill walk again. The children wanted to show their mum and dad the bird-shooting butt and see if it had been

filled in, but the first thing they saw on the walk was
another new sign:

FARM LIVESTOCK
TO AVOID DISTURBING FARM LIVESTOCK
PLEASE KEEP DOGS UNDER CLOSE CONTROL
AND PREFERABLY ON A LEAD.

RESERVOIR ZOMBIES

Introduction

In 1935, to provide water for Manchester, a reservoir was created by building a big dam in the beautiful lake of Haweswater in Cumbria, making it over three times its natural size. The tiny village of Mardale Green, including its church, was flooded in the process, and farmers had to abandon their homes and hundreds of acres of land.

This was to be Joe's final visit to the abandoned village. In just a few weeks it would disappear under the new reservoir. As the old shepherd walked sadly down familiar lanes through the village, an eerie stillness surrounded the place. There was no sign of any human life and the cattle and sheep were already moved to new pastures. The hedgerows, now untrimmed, were sprouting everywhere with wild flowers, enjoying their freedom to grow, as if they knew what was to come.

He came to the Dun Bull, the inn which for centuries had been a favourite place of many a weary shepherd and farmworker. It was here that he came for a well-earned drink and pie supper after a hard day on the hills. He paused a while, remembering how it had been only a few years ago: the bar room with its sturdy oak beams and open fireplace, himself with other shepherds and farmers laughing and swapping tales with the local people, jolly folk at the bar and the cheers when the delicious home-cooked food was served. The inn, which was still visited by the ghosts of the regular customers from over the years, would now vanish under the lake. He walked on feeling like a stranger, here where he had lived and worked all his life. The birds' loud songs somehow made the silent village seem even quieter. It was the sound of death. Mardale Green was doomed.

Even his old friends resting in the graveyard of the tiny church had not been left in peace. For years, unknown to Joe, their ghosts had enjoyed revisiting the Dun Bull. When the earthly folks of Mardale Green had finished their nightly business, the ghostly forms of Jake Thackery, Fred Davis, Ernie Godwin and Bill Woods would appear at the dead of night. They'd meet like old friends, haunting the bar, chatting until dawn as they had done in life. But now their graves had been dug open and their coffins moved to another burial ground five miles away, at the village of Shap, where there was nothing for them and they did not feel at home.

Over fifty years had now passed, and the four old Mardale friends grew increasingly restless in their new graves. Like all ghosts, they only wanted to haunt the village in which they had lived. Eventually, the driest summer in England for decades gave them their opportunity. With their ghostly senses they knew this was the time to get back to Mardale.

At the darkest hour of the summer night, just before dawn, using one of the most powerful forces available to a spirit, they climbed back into their bodies and became zombies.

One by one they clambered out of their graves, staggering about learning to walk again and balance on old legs that had not been used for years. And with the bright moonlight to guide them, they became the walking dead. Looking up at the church tower they recognised the weather vane; like them, it had been moved to Shap from the small church in Mardale. It was still telling the way of the wind just as it did fifty years ago.

They headed west across familiar fields and farmland and nothing much had changed. Their path led them across deserted moorland on to the old corpse route. This track was used to transport the Mardale dead to Shap years ago, before a piece of ground in Mardale was set aside to be used for burial. Slowly the four old friends shuffled along as the sun rose, each still with the same problems they had when they were alive. Jake with his shaky hip managed with a new stick he ripped from a tree along the way. Fred walked with only one arm swinging by his side; his other arm was lost in the Great War. Ernie, his eyesight not improved over the years in a grave, latched on to Fred's good arm. Bill's deafness and bursts of uncontrolled shaking, both due to things that happened in the Great War, had come before an early death, but his eyes were still just as good as a young man's eyes, and so he led the way.

As they trudged along they heard the sad-sounding cry of the curlew as it flew over the moors where it nested. On the ground they were ignored by sheep grazing the moor as they had done for hundreds of years. They had not travelled far when, to their dismay, they spotted some early-morning walkers coming towards them. They did not want to be recognised as anything other than living, normal people. Their main focus was to return to Mardale and their old haunting ground.

'Morning', one of the walkers said as the zombies passed. 'Heading for Patterdale?'

Bill, having one of his trembly moments, let out a moan. The others managed to mumble between them, 'Aye Patterdale, Patterdale, that's it … '

They did not stop to chat and continued hobbling along their way. In the early morning twilight they looked like some old timers, weary after completing an overnight journey. None of them had any backpacks but they hoped the hillwalkers didn't suspect anything sinister in the way they looked.

Before long, towards the end of the old corpse

road, an awesome sight came before them. Instead of looking down on the village that was once their home, they saw the reservoir spread out before them. Although they had known the fate of Mardale Green, the sight of the lake in the early morning light overwhelmed them. Speechless, they stumbled down the track towards it. They could now see the stone walls of Chapel Bridge as well as the walls that bordered the old lanes coming out from the reservoir, uncovered by the recent drought. But the dry weather alone had not reduced the lake to the level they needed in order to get into the inn. The zombies knew that to allow access to the Dun Bull, the lake would have to lose a lot more water. Somehow they would have to make a hole in the reservoir dam.

Arriving down at the lake, they took the new road above the shore, walking away from the village and towards the dam. They paid little attention to the new hotel, built as a replacement for the old inn where they really longed to be.

They soon arrived at the dam. Having come so far, they were not going to let a fence and a few trees on the sloping hillside stop them now. With their spirits uplifted, eagerness overcame their old, tired bodies and they scrambled clumsily over the fence. Down the bank they slid, grabbing trees to break their fall. Eventually they arrived at the valve house, from where the water in the reservoir was controlled. Bill knew what they needed to do from his time in the Great War. Technology had changed but the basics were the same. Breaking into the tool room, they grabbed what was needed. They found some workmen's jackets, so they put them on to help disguise themselves. Smashing off the locks with a big hammer, they swung on the valve wheel and eventually it came loose. Water gushed into the stream below, which until now had been just a trickle; they even started to hear waterfalls nearby. It was still early in the morning and hours to go before the workers who looked after the dam would realise what had happened.

With their task now done, water was fast draining out of the reservoir and more of the village was beginning to appear out of the water. It was time for the four friends to make their way back down the road. More early morning walkers ignored them, as they were wearing the workmen's jackets and so no one suspected a thing. Knowing exactly where to look, the four zombies could see the old walls of the Dun Bull Inn starting to emerge from the water. The old inn floor was now covered by only a few ripples in the lake.

The old friends sat down. One lit a fire in the great fireplace, and there they chatted, waiting perhaps for some lovely food to be served from the kitchen, maybe even a drink to be served from the bar. Happy they were, talking once again about the good old days. As they grew tired, they thought of their beds. Removing a stone slab from the floor, they climbed down into the inn's cellar. Hidden in one corner they opened a door to a secret passage known only to the spirit world.

Scrambling through the narrow tunnel to the church graveyard, they completed their journey and laid their old bodies to rest in their original burial place. The zombies were now dead to the world again, but their spirits were free to roam the underwater village of Mardale Green and enjoy their nights haunting the Dun Bull once again.

Eventually, when the dam was repaired and the drought came to an end, Mardale Green completely disappeared under the waters once more. But if you ever see the walls of the old lanes and Chapel Bridge rise up out of the lake, think of those four ghosts of Mardale who are content to remain in the underwater village. And if you can hear the waterfalls of Thornthwaite Force during the summer, you may wonder – have more of their friends arrived from Shap?

With special thanks to: Liz for her love and encouragement, my good friend Judith who skilfully perfected my writing, and my editors Jon Barton and Camilla Barnard at Vertebrate who crafted my words into this book.